# The Funky Frecks

## Jennifer Gilmour

To Chris,
Thank you for backing the
kickstarter campaign resulting
in the publication of the
Funky Frecks. Without you
it may not have been possible.
Together we are Louder!
Jennifer
Gilmour

# The Funky Frecks

First published in 2023 Jennifer Gilmour
Copyright © 2023 Jennifer Gilmour
All rights reserved. No part of this book may be reproduced or transmitted in any form or by any means, electronic or mechanical, including photocopying, recording, or by any information and retrieval system, without the author's permission.
A CIP catalogue record for this book is available from the British Library.
ISBN: 978-1-9999647-3-3 (Neilson UK)

Cover Copyright ©Jennifer Gilmour
Published by Pict Publishing

# DEDICATION

This book is dedicated to my three children, Sophie, Riley & Robyn, you were the reason I brought this to life. May all your relationships be full of trust, love and balance.

# ACKNOWLEDGEMENTS

Thank you first to Emma Mitchell from Creating Perfection who has spent the time to edit and offer her insight into this book.

Second, thank you to Georgina Preston for her illustrative work on the cover and the artistic direction of the illustrations throughout the book, taking my visions and bringing them to life.

Thank you to the book bloggers who help spread the word about my new releases and all my news. Your support on social media helps the message reach more people and you are a vital part of helping me raise awareness.

Thank you to my fellow authors who continue to inspire and motivate me to continue my journey.

Proofreader: Emily Woodcock

Beta Readers: Tracey Driver and Erin Buck

Your feedback was reassuring in the later stages of the book coming together. Thank you for your time.

Thank you to my top Patron, Dana Lemaster for the mass of support I receive on Twitter.

Thank you to those who supported the birth of this book by pledging in the Kickstarter campaign which took place in Oct/Nov 2021. Without your support this book wouldn't have come to life. A full list of supporters can be found at the back of this book.

Thank you to official partners of the book:

NCDV

DV-ACT

Kaleidoscopic UK

Free Spirit Cambs

These charities work tirelessly to help people in need and details of each one can be found in the back.

And finally, thank you, the reader. Without you, none of this would be possible. So sit back, relax, and come and meet Jess as she embarks on a *huge* adventure!

# CONTENTS

# The Funky Frecks

# THE NEW SCHOOL

The sun crept through a gap in the curtains and shone onto Jess's face.

'Mmmm,' Jess murmured. She didn't want to get up, and gripping onto the warm covers, she rolled over.

Tap…tap…tap…the knocking came again.

'Argh,' Jess grunted again.

'Come on, Jess, it's your first day, you can't be late.' Her mum raised her voice as she walked to Jack's bedroom to wake him up too.

Jess opened one eye to see what time it was.

8:00 a.m.!

Jess jumped out of bed and started getting ready.

'Mum! Why didn't you wake me up earlier?'

'I did try,' she shouted from down the hall.

Jess had wanted today to be perfect. It was her first day at a new school and she wanted to make a good impression.

Her navy-blue blazer with a golden anchor on the right of the chest hung in her wardrobe next to the perfectly ironed shirt and grey skirt.

Rushing to get ready she almost fell over as she pulled her socks up. Then the excitement set in and the butterflies in her tummy woke up.

In the kitchen ten minutes later, Jess joined her brother Jack at the table where he was already tucking into a bowl of Coco Pops. Jack giggled as Jess sat down, his mousy brown hair was spiked up and Jess couldn't help thinking how cool he was. So much cooler than she was.

She scrunched her face up as she poured out her own cereal and began to shovel it in one spoon after the other.

'It's OK, darling, you have time to eat normally. I'm driving you in today, as it's your first day. Don't rush your food,' their mum said.

Jack rolled his eyes and scrunched his freckle-covered nose.

Jess had freckles too, but she hated hers. She knew she looked different to everyone else. She had long white hair which swung all the way down her back. It was so white that people often stopped and stared at her. Then they'd notice her eyes; one green and the other brown. She hated how mismatched she was.

She didn't just have blonde hair, she had white hair.

She didn't have nice green or brown eyes; she had one green and one brown eye.

At her last school, the other students had called her all sorts of names and she came to hate the way she looked.

But this was a fresh start. A new school and new friends.

Things would be different now, she was sure.

# THE NEW FRIEND

Mum took them to the reception desk and introduced them.

'Hello, Sergeant Davies, Jess, and Jack,' the receptionist said. 'It's great to have you here.'

Jess loved that her mum was so important. She was in the army which meant they had to move around a lot, but now she had a new role at the local barracks, and they were hoping they would be staying here for a long time. Michelle, the receptionist, buzzed Jess and Jack through the security door and told them to come along so she could take them to their classrooms. After they'd said goodbye to their mum, they walked through, and Jess grabbed Jack's hand.

'Don't worry,' he said. 'I'll see you in the playground at break time…you're going to be fine.' He knew how nervous she was. She watched him walk towards his classroom and felt all alone. Those butterflies were going crazy in her stomach now. Michelle guided her down the corridor and when she opened the door to the right classroom, the sound of laughter filled her ears.

The teacher stood at the front of the room and the children were all laughing their heads off. Miss Antcliffe had brown curly hair, which was tied back with a pink ribbon, and her dress was covered in brightly coloured flowers, butterflies, and birds. She was smiling and her cheeks were rosy. Jess didn't think she'd seen actual rosy cheeks on an adult before.

When she saw Jess and Michelle, Miss Antcliffe asked the class to settle down.

'Everyone, we have a new student today.' She beckoned Jess over to the front next to her desk.

Jess's stomach lurched. Every time she started a new school, she had to do this. The introduction.

'Hi, my name is Jess and we've just moved here because my mum's in the army. I like unicorns, crafting, Roblox, and I have a brother called Jack in Year Six.' Jess glanced back at Miss Antcliffe, hoping that was enough.

'Thank you, Jess. Isn't that lovely, everyone? I think we have quite a few students who like unicorns and play Roblox too. So, who wants to buddy up with Jess this week? This is a special job to show her around, help her settle in…who would like to be her unicorn-loving buddy?'

A girl at the front with jet-black hair in a short bob and dazzling blue eyes was the first to put her hand up, straining to get it higher. She had a huge smile on her face, and Jess thought she looked nice and fun.

A couple of others put their hands up, but it was clear who wanted to buddy up the most.

'Fantastic, thank you, everyone. I think Sam was the first to put her hand up and looks particularly enthusiastic. So…Jess…meet Sam.'

'Hi,' the girls said in unison before grinning at each other.

Miss Antcliffe moved a couple of the students around so she could sit next to Sam, and then the class continued. Jess had a feeling everything was going to be just fine.

Sam was hilarious, and she knew everyone!

'Have you met Jess yet, Mrs Richards?' she said to the headteacher when they went out to the playground at break time.

'Mr Petch!' she shouted. 'This is the new girl, Jess. Jess, Mr Petch is the PE teacher.' Mr Petch waved at them from the dinner line at lunchtime.

At the end of the day, they linked arms and walked out to the playground where Jess was meeting Jack to walk home. She'd had a great day and couldn't wait to tell her mum.

Around the dinner table that night, Jess told her mum and dad all about her new friend. How hilarious she was and how they'd spent the whole day giggling. Jack had a great day, too. He was going to join the football team.

After tea, they both asked if they could have some extra time on their tablets to join their new friends in a Roblox game. Luckily, mum and dad agreed, and they rushed to the sofa together. That night, Jess went to sleep with a huge smile on her face.

The next morning Jess woke with a spring in her step; filled with excitement about what today would be like. Greeting her mum, dad, and Jack with a smile, she sat down for breakfast. Today, there were no butterflies flapping around.

She and Jack walked to school and before she had the chance to be nervous in the playground, she heard Sam.

'Hiiiiii, Jeeeessssss!!!!' she shouted at the top of her voice.

'Bye, Jack,' Jess said, as she walked confidently with Sam into school. Jack was happy to see her so settled. There was only a year between them, and they were close. Jack had hated how nervous she'd been, so he was glad that she'd found a friend so quickly.

# THE RED FLAG

That afternoon, Jess's class were teamed up to draw portraits of each other. She was so excited to get her new art supplies out. Whenever she started a new school her parents bought her new stationery, and this time she had a unicorn themed set, as well as brand-new felt tips and colouring pencils.

She lined the pencils and felt tips up in a neat row, then added her unicorn ruler and eraser to the line.

'Ooooh…I love those!' Sam squealed. 'They're so pretty. Can I use them too?' Sam asked.

The butterflies Jess thought had disappeared returned to her tummy. At her old school, her 'best friend' had 'borrowed' her things all the time. The only problem was, Jess never got them back. Or if she did, they'd been ruined. She really didn't want that to happen again, but she desperately wanted Sam to be her friend.

'Yes, of course you can,' she stammered.

Sam threw her arm around Jess's shoulder and said, 'Cheers, Frecks.'

Jess shuddered. She never thought she'd hear that name again!

'I don't like that name, Sam.' She moved away from Sam's hug. 'The kids at my old school used to call me it…they…made fun of me.'

Jess was sure Sam would understand, but still held her breath while she waited for her to answer.

'Oh, Jess! I'm so sorry! I love your freckles and I just wanted to give you a nickname to help you feel more at home here.'

Jess felt really guilty then, so she threw her arms around Sam and then pushed her supplies to the middle of the table.

'Let's get drawing,' she said with a big grin on her face.

That afternoon she went along to the playtime sports club with Sam.

Mr Petch was putting the students into teams when Sam shouted, 'Sir, I have to be in the same as Frecks…I'm her school buddy and she needs me…don't you, Frecks?'

Jess was horrified. Everyone looked at her, and she could feel her facing burning. She just knew her freckles would be glowing for everyone to see.

And now that Sam had used that name in front of everyone, she was worried they'd all start calling her it, too.

As playtime continued, Jess thought about and realised it was probably a mistake. Sam knew she didn't like the name, so it must have been an accident.

When she explained what had happened to her mum that night, she agreed. Jess went to bed feeling a little better and just hoped that no one would call her Frecks tomorrow.

# A FRIENDLY FACE

In maths the next day, Jess was teamed up with Victoria.

Jess thought Victoria looked kind and when she'd heard her laughing with her friends she wanted to join in, but Sam had steered them away from her. She was glad to be able to spend time with someone else.

Victoria had hair the colour of fire and bright green's eyes. Jess couldn't help wishing she had two bright green eyes, too. And as she looked closer, she noticed something else.

Victoria had freckles. Hundreds of them! Just like hers.

They worked through their maths problems together and made a great team. Then Victoria told her about the craft club at lunchtime. Jess was so excited. She told Victoria about the pen pot she'd made, and Victoria told her about the jewellery box she'd made. They spent the rest of the lesson laughing, and when she glanced over at Sam, Jess couldn't believe how angry she looked.

Surely it was about the maths and not her being with Victoria...wasn't it?

Sam wasn't at craft club and Jess felt herself smile a little harder when she realised.

She sat with Victoria, and they got started on a new project together.

'You didn't like it when Sam called you Frecks, did you?'

Jess was shocked. How did Victoria know that? She didn't know what to say. Sam was her friend; it was only an accident. She didn't want Victoria to think she was mad with Sam, but she didn't want her to think it was OK to call her it either.

'Erm…actually…'

'It's OK, I get called it too.' Victoria gave her a tight smile. 'I hated it, but now I just tell them my freckles are glittering and they're just jealous they don't have any.'

They fell into fits of giggles.

'If you want, we could start a club,' Victoria said. 'The Funky Frecks!'

'I love it!' Jess said. And with that, she relaxed again. Sam was nice, but it felt different being friends with Victoria. Like she really understood her.

Back in the classroom, Jess was seated with Sam again. She felt awkward this time, though.

'I missed you at lunchtime,' Sam said grumpily.

Jess told her where she'd been.

'That's OK, can we stick together tomorrow, though? Victoria is really clingy, like a bad smell that won't go away.' Sam started giggling.

'Yeah, I suppose so. I'm not sure what clubs are on though.'

'It doesn't matter, we will go to them together. Just us, like before.' Sam put her arm around Jess's shoulder and pulled her close and all of a sudden, those butterflies came back.

'Victoria is a bit strange, you know?' Sam said as they walked into class.

Jess didn't know what to say, so she gave a nervous nod. Victoria didn't seem strange. In fact, she seemed to be just like her. They had tried to say hello to each other that morning, but Sam had dragged Jess in the opposite direction, and she wouldn't leave her side. It was the same for the rest of the week.

# THINGS DON'T FEEL RIGHT

When the weekend finally arrived, Mum knew there was something wrong with Jess.

They spent some time together as a family and finally, on Saturday afternoon, once the boys had gone to play football, they were alone.

'You know I can tell when something's wrong, darling, and I know there's something on your mind. Do you want to talk about it while we make some cupcakes?'

Jess nodded, and while her mum got the baking things out, she explained what had happened with Sam and Victoria.

'The main problem is, I want to be friends with them both, but I just know Sam will be hurt if I say I want to spend time with Victoria. I tried to be nice to her when she called me Frecks and I thought she understood me, but she clearly didn't coz she carried on calling me it. I just don't know what to do.'

'Well, darling. You just need to tell her again. Still be kind but tell her that you wanting to be friends with Victoria doesn't mean you don't want to be friends with her too. I'm certain she will understand.'

Jess wasn't so sure, and by Sunday night the butterflies had come back again.

As Jess and Jack approached the school gates on Monday morning, Victoria was waving at them with one hand and in the other she had a sheet of poster paper.

She'd spent all weekend working on a club logo for Jess and she couldn't wait to show her it. Just as they got close enough to speak, Sam bounded over and grabbed Jess's arm.

'We can't talk,' she said to Victoria. 'We're late.' And she started to pull Jess away.

'Hang on, I like Victoria,' Jess said. 'I can be friends with you both.'

Sam tutted and shook her head.

'I'm older than you, Jess, and I care about you. You're my best friend. Victoria is weird and I don't want to play with her. Come on.' And with that, she dragged her towards the entrance.

By break time, Jess had decided she wasn't going to give in.

Victoria was waiting to show Jess her the club logo. On it they had glittery specks for their freckles, they were dressed like superheroes, and she'd written *The Funky Frecks* around it.

'Sam, I know you don't like Victoria, but I want to be friends with both of you. Do you want to play with us?'

'No way! Why would I want to go anywhere near her?!' Sam was really angry this time. 'If you want to be her friend, go ahead, but we won't be friends anymore.'

Jess had thought she could handle this, but now she didn't know what to do. How could she be friends with both of them without the other one being hurt?

As the week went on, Sam got to her before she had the chance to go to Victoria and soon, it was clear to her that she couldn't be friends with both girls.

'Come on, Frecks,' Sam would say.

'What shall we do now, Frecks?'

Jess was stuck.

She just couldn't see a way of getting through to Sam.

# THE GUILTY FEELING

Jess arrived at school on Monday a few weeks later determined to be strong with Sam. In the playground, Jack rushed off to meet his friends and almost as soon as he'd gone, Sam was by her side.

'Did you have a good weekend?' Jess asked.

'Yeah...but I spent all my pocket money. How much do you get? I get five pounds.'

'I get the same,' Jess said. 'I'm saving up, though, so I didn't spend any of mine.'

'Oh, that's brilliant! I need some more money to...erm...help my cousin. If you give me some of yours, I won't tell Victoria what you said about her.'

'What...I...sai—'

'Yes, remember, when you said she was needy...if you give me your money, I won't tell her about it.' Sam looked at Jess with a big grin on her face.

Jess felt sick. She hadn't said that…had she? She tried to think back to the conversation as Sam linked her arm through hers and guided her towards to the school door. She glanced around the playground and saw Victoria smiling at her. She couldn't let Sam tell her anything nasty. She would be so hurt.

'OK…I'll, I'll bring you it in tomorrow.'

Sam grinned again. 'You're the best friend ever, Jess.'

# MAKING EXCUSES

A few weeks later, Miss Antcliffe asked Jess to stay in the classroom at the end of the day. She came and sat on one of the chairs at Jess's table and looked straight at her.

'You've been with us for a few weeks now, Jess. How are you settling in?'

Jess squirmed in her seat.

'Erm…OK…have I done something wrong?'

'Not at all,' Miss Antcliffe replied. 'You're doing well in your classes and the clubs you've joined, but I couldn't help but notice that you stopped going to craft club and that you don't sit with Victoria anymore. I thought you two had formed a new friendship club?'

Jess wanted to cry thinking about the poster Victoria had made.

'Oh, that...that was just kid stuff.'

Jess knew Sam would be waiting in the corridor for her, and she didn't want her to hear anything about this. She'd been giving Sam half of her pocket money for a few weeks now, and she didn't want Sam to get jealous and start threatening to tell Victoria what she'd said again.

'Victoria is a bit worried about you, Jess. She thinks you aren't doing the things you want to do because Sam doesn't like to do them.'

'That's just…erm…silly. Sam's my, erm…she's my best friend.'

Miss Antcliffe looked over the top of her glasses at Jess with a look that said, *who are you kidding*?

'Well, I'm here if you ever need to talk, OK?'

As Jess stood to leave, she hoped desperately that Sam had believed her words, otherwise, she thought things were about to get much worse.

# THE SECRET

That night, Jess lay on her bed crying. She'd thought Victoria hated her for ignoring her over the last few weeks, but she mustn't do if she'd spoken to the teacher. With this thought in her head, she felt brave and strong and before she could change her mind, she grabbed her phone and called Victoria.

'Thank you for thinking about me, but please don't worry, I'm OK. Please don't say anything to Miss Antcliffe again, though. The thing is…I…I think I said something to Sam about you on my first day. I really don't remember saying anything. I was just nodding and agreeing with what she was saying. I didn't know what to say to her…it was awkward.

'But then she saw your poster and got jealous and said she'd tell you everything if I didn't share my pocket money with her and I didn't want you to think I'd been mean about you, so I agreed. I want to be your friend, but I don't know what to do and I don't think talking to anyone is going to help. Mum suggested I talk to Sam, but that didn't work.

'And today, Sam was outside the classroom when Miss Antcliffe spoke to me. It's like she's always there and I can't get away from her. But I don't want you to think I said anything about you. I'm really really really sure I didn't say it. I just nodded. Which is just as bad—'

'Jess!' Victoria interrupted. 'That's awful—'

'Oh no!' Jess said suddenly. 'Victoria, I don't believe this…Sam is here…My mum's just shouted me.

'Hang on…I've got to go.'

'She's coming upstairs!'

Jess put the phone down and threw herself back on the bed just as Sam bounced through the bedroom door.

'Hi, Jess. My mum's in the car outside. I wanted to check on our project and look at your half so I can match it to mine at home.'

Sam looked around her bedroom and turned her nose up at the bright pink walls and JoJo Siwa posters. She'd been to Jess's house once before, but not in her bedroom, as it was still being decorated after they'd moved.

'Oh, you're a JoJo fan? That's so babyish.'

Sam did an impression of JoJo and took the mick out of her.

'I really can't believe you like her, Jess. I think I need to help you grow up.'

Jess was so embarrassed and knew her cheeks would be flaming. She was getting fed up with Sam making her feel this way.

'What do you want, Sam?'

'I need that pocket money. You didn't bring it to school this week and I'm going to see my cousin, so yeah, I need it now.'

Jess went to one of the bags hanging on the back of her door and rummaged around.

'I've only got five-pound notes. I don't think my mum will give me any change this time.'

'Don't worry, Frecks. I'll just take that.'

Jess flinched at the nickname Sam refused to stop using.

'Thanks, Frecks. See you tomorrow,' Sam said as she made her way downstairs.

'Thanks for doing *some* of the project. I suppose *I'll* have to finish it off tonight.'

She got to the bottom of the stairs just as Sam slammed the front door shut. Jess's mum stared at her with a mixture of concern and worry on her face, but before she could say anything, Jess ran back to her room.

She tried to call Victoria back, but there was no answer.

*No wonder*, she thought, *she probably hates me now she knows what I did.*

Jess laid on her bed looking around and, as the tears started to fall, she jumped up in anger and tore the JoJo Siwa posters from the walls.

As the last poster ripped the paint off, she heard her mum calling her downstairs again. Her stomach dropped. Was Sam back?

# THE RELIEF

Jess couldn't believe it when she got to the kitchen. Sat around the breakfast bar with her mum was Victoria and her mum. Jess burst into tears.

Victoria jumped up and pulled her into a hug. 'It's OK,' she whispered, and wiped Jess's tears away with her sleeve.

Victoria's mum started. 'Kath,' she said, looking at Jess's mum. 'I'm sorry to say I overheard a conversation between these two earlier and it seems we have a problem.'

*This is it*, thought Jess. *I'm going to be in so much trouble for being such a horrible person.*

Then, before she knew it, Victoria and her mum were explaining how Sam had been bullying and manipulating Jess. How she'd been coming between the two friends for no reason other than jealously. How Jess has tried her hardest to be a good friend but was being pressured to be something else. Her tears were falling harder and harder until Victoria handed her a folded-up piece of paper...

Jess opened it and finally saw *The Funky Frecks* logo in all its glory.

It was bright and cheery and spoke about friendship. Victoria had added a motto underneath the logo.

*The Funky Frecks are friends who share freckles, fun and crafts, and who be what they want to be!*

When her mum asked why she hadn't told her this was all going on, Jess explained she thought she could handle it herself.

'Well, it seems that you Funky Frecks need to realise that it's OK to make mistakes, as long as you own up to them. You have a whole team of people to support you, don't forget that.'

Victoria's mum joined in.

'As long as you are happy and safe, you will be fine. Keep on caring for each other, girls. I'm very proud of what you've both done about this situation. Jess, you tried to protect your friend, and Victoria, you were able to speak out when your friend couldn't. You are both amazing.'

Jess and Victoria pulled each other closer for another hug. 'All we need now is to glitter paint our freckles!' Jess said as they tumbled to the floor in a fit of giggles.

# THE SUPPORT OF OTHERS

The next day, Jess and her mum went to school and spoke with Miss Antcliffe. She was shocked how bad things had got but was determined to sort things out once and for all.

Instead of making it obvious that Jess's mum had been involved, Miss Antcliffe decided to do a special swap day. She asked all the children to move seats and sit with someone they hadn't ever sat with before. Then she did some work with the whole class on friendships.

They talked about how many friends you can have. Where you can find friends. That it's OK to have school friends, friends from your family, friends on the street where you live, and friends at clubs you go to outside school. They also talked about how it's OK to spend time with your friends on your own, or as part of a group.

Miss Antcliffe asked the children to get into groups to make friendship posters. Jess and Victoria knew what they were going to do. They got all the supplies they needed, marched over to where Sam was sitting on her own, plonked their things on the table, and sat down.

Jess looked her in the eyes and said, 'I am your friend, Sam. No matter what. But I am Victoria's friend too. Now, you can join us, or you can be on your own. What do you want to do?'

Sam stared at her and then Victoria for a moment, and then slowly, a smile appeared on her face.

When they'd finished drawing themselves on their poster, Victoria and Jess looked at Sam's picture, then, before she could stop them, they added her a sprinkle of glitter freckles before laughing and giggling.

'Welcome to The Funky Frecks!'

# FOR YOU, READER

This is for all you potential *Funky Frecks Club Members*!

Do you have a friendship group that has a club motto? What did you think of *The Funky Frecks* motto?

The Funky Frecks are friends who share freckles, fun and crafts, and who be what they want to be!

Just for fun, take a moment and think about what your motto would be for your friendship group. You could even doodle your own logo to showcase the personality of your group.

*The Funky Frecks* are open for club members.

All you have to do is embrace who you are and be who you want to be. This gives you automatic entry. Jess, Victoria, and Sam would be more than happy to welcome you in.

# FOR PARENTS, TEACHERS, COMMUNITY WORKERS, CHILDREN, AND YOUTH WORKERS

## FREE RESOURCES

The vision of this book was to help our younger generation better understand the difference between healthy friendships and unhealthy friendships with the vision of it being a prevention.

Download your free resource pack to use in the classroom, youth groups or at home with your own children.

The pack explains the vision of the book further and how it can be used to explore children's choices of friendships in a healthy way.

What's included in the pack:

- Two activities with printable sheets
- Discussion questions

- About the author
- Further resources

Head to: www.jennifergilmour.com/the-funky-frecks-resources/

If there are any problems accessing the link or downloading the pack, please contact me directly at: contact@jennifergilmour.com

# PARTNERS

Thank you to those that have partnered with *The Funky Frecks* all of which offer a valuable service to the domestic abuse sector. Please spend some time learning about them and how they can help the families you may work with.

## NCDV

The National Centre for Domestic Violence offers a free, fast emergency injunction service to victims and survivors of domestic abuse and violence, regardless of their financial circumstances, race, gender, or sexual orientation. Our award-winning free service allows anyone who has recently suffered or been threatened with domestic abuse or violence to apply for an emergency court injunction.

This can sometimes be issued within twenty-four hours of making contact with us. We work in close partnership with the police, solicitors and other support agencies (Refuge, Women's Aid, etc.) to help victims obtain speedy protection.

www.ncdv.org.uk

## DV-ACT

DV-ACT is an organisation that works with cases where children are in danger due to abuse in the home and the courts are involved. We provide risk assessments and treatment programmes to parents in child protection measures and training and consultancy around domestic and sexual abuse to local authorities and professionals. Visit our website at dvact.org to find out more.

www.dvact.org

## KALEIDOSCOPIC UK

Kaleidoscopic UK is a peer support charity for those subjected to any form of domestic abuse past or present. We provide open-ended and threshold free survivor- led support groups, coffee mornings and trauma-informed recovery programmes for all. We deliver prevention/education programmes for children and those that support them in England and Wales (Eductae2Eradictae) which can be delivered in group settings. We educate and inform voluntary and statutory services, as well as the public at large, about all forms of domestic abuse and its harmful effects through the eyes of survivors, removing the taboo and implementing positive change.

www.kaleidoscopic.uk

## Free Spirit Cambs

At Free Spirit Cambs, our aim is to empower those affected by domestic abuse and give them the tools to rebuild their lives. We provide a safe environment to gain information, support, and to speak without fear. We believe that although domestic abuse is gendered, disproportionately affecting women, with men being the perpetrators, anyone can fall victim to domestic abuse. We offer workshops/courses that support women, children, and men regardless of their gender or sexuality.

www.freespiritcambs.wixsite.com/women

# THANK YOU

## TO THE FOLLOWING PEOPLE WHO PLEDGED THEIR SUPPORT:

Beat Mueller

Becka Simm

Bob Bennett

Chris Green

Courtney Farrow of Bloom Creative

Debbie Mawer

Dr Mandeep Kaur Khela

Edd Withers

Heidi Thomas

HMB Training Services

Kelly Owen

Lilyth Coglan

Michala Leyland Wood for the Trees Coaching

Mum

National Centre For Domestic Violence CIC

Pablito Greco

Paramedic Chris book series
(www.timparsons.co.uk)

Paul Weatherill

Puzzle Piece Law

Richard Graham Judd

Robin Gilmour

Stephanie Jane Home Alignment Specialist

Sue Wickstead (Lego Lady) JayJayBooks

Tamsin Cain SM ACCPH

The Creative Fund by BackerKit

The Dyslexic Dyslexia Consultant

Tracy Rector

Vivien Bickham

# ABOUT THE AUTHOR

Jennifer Gilmour is an author and advocate for women in abusive relationships, using her own experiences of domestic abuse as a catalyst to bring awareness and to help others. Jennifer has published two works, Isolation Junction and Clipped Wings, which have both been Amazon Best Sellers and received awards. Jennifer speaks at events across the UK and continues to raise awareness through blog posts, public speaking, radio interviews, and social media.

Jennifer has listened to her readers and has grown a digital community to support discussions about domestic abuse online. Starting with her Twitter Chat #AbuseTalk, which opened late 2017, this developed into an online forum in 2018. In

2019, Jennifer launched a podcast which includes interviews with those in the sector and gives followers the opportunity to ask burning questions.

Most Informative Blogger Award 2018 (Bloggers Bash Annual Awards)

UK & European Award for using Social Media for Good 2019 (Social Day: Social Media Marketing Awards)

Small Business Sunday Winner 2020 (Theo Paphitis #SBS)

Jennifer says: "Together we are *louder*"

@JenLGilmour

JenniferGilmour.com

# ALSO FROM JENNIFER GILMOUR

## ISOLATION JUNCTION

100 reasons to leave, 1,000 reasons to stay.

When Rose married the love of her life, she was expecting the perfect family life she'd always dreamt of, but before her first child was born her husband, Darren, changed.

Almost overnight, Rose's life is turned upside down and the life she'd envisioned seemed like an impossible dream.

As Darren's abuse deepens, Rose has 100 reasons to leave but thousands why she can't. Will she ever escape the hellish life she and her children are trapped in?

Can Rose stop her life spiralling further out of control?

Can she find the life she desperately wants for her children?

Stuck at *Isolation Junction*, which way will Rose turn?

## CLIPPED WINGS

The silent chorus.

Just imagine you thought that you had met the man or woman of your dreams. This person was charming, and you thought they were the one or perhaps that this was fate; it was just meant to be.

But as the months go by things, start to change. Their behaviour towards you isn't the same. They are more critical, more particular about your appearance, what you do, how you do it, who you see.

Time goes by and you feel isolated from your friends and family because that behaviour has now changed to threats, maybe violence and you feel that your identity is all but gone. But still you stay. Where would you go? Who would help you? You are not worthy.

But you are.

A group of survivors have spoken about their own experiences. In their own words, they show that survivors do have a voice and that it needs to be heard. They show that abuse isn't unique or strange but that it is, unfortunately, a surprisingly common problem in today's society.

The message of this book is one of courage, as with courage comes awareness and an ability to understand what has happened to you and take the steps needed to become a survivor yourself.

Printed in Great Britain
by Amazon

22182787R00040